KO•EMS

Zen Koan Meets Child's Poem

miller & muse

STORIES and SONGS for the SPIRITUALLY CURIOUS

INTRODUCTION

KO-EMS combine the essence of the austere Zen KOAN—*What is the sound of one hand clapping?*—with the playful innocence of a children's POEM—*Jack Sprat could eat no fat...*

The result is two rhyming couplets that can both twist your mind and bring a smile.

Happy contemplation.

DEDICATION

TO MARIANNE, for decades of love, support and adventure.

It's been a long journey on roads—paved and unpaved, external and internal—filled with unexpected detours, discoveries and transformations.

May it continue.

Credits

Text and illustrations by the author:
© 2024-2025 William Eugene Miller.
All rights reserved.

Back cover photograph:
Matt Vielle, Hamilton Studio.
Spokane WA.

3D Yin-Yang symbol:
PhotoShop AI.

Printed in the USA:
On-demand by
Amazon KDP
and IngramSpark.

Published by

STORIES and SONGS for the SPIRITUALLY CURIOUS

Follow Bodhi Bill

BodhiBill.com

TABLE *of* CONTENTS

POEM 3
KOEM 16
KOEM 23
KO·EMS
KOEM 7
KOEM 20
KOEM 2
KOEM 14
KOEM 21

You can read

   this book

With just a

   single look.

But savor

   every rhyme,

It lasts a long,

   long time.

Sadly, the song
sang on
After the music
was gone.
Some hoped she'd
sing it again,
But poor Sadly
never knew when.

B J X Q N K T E G H S W
C Y V M L V K L

Once upon

a twice

Never sounds

as nice

As when it was

a word

Still waiting

to be heard.

Little Miss Smithey
went to the fair

Only to find herself
already there.

Bewildered, she left and
went home because

She'd much rather be
where she already was.

Tuttle, the tutor,
would talk

Just like his
grandfather's clock.

But then, after he
had unwound,

He'd speak without
making a sound.

Guinn came in

to leave,

Or so I do

believe.

The facts are not

so clear

As Guinn is still

not here.

Funny was
	sad today.

Yesterday'd
	gone away.

Tomorrow would
	go as well.

But where, Funny
	never could tell.

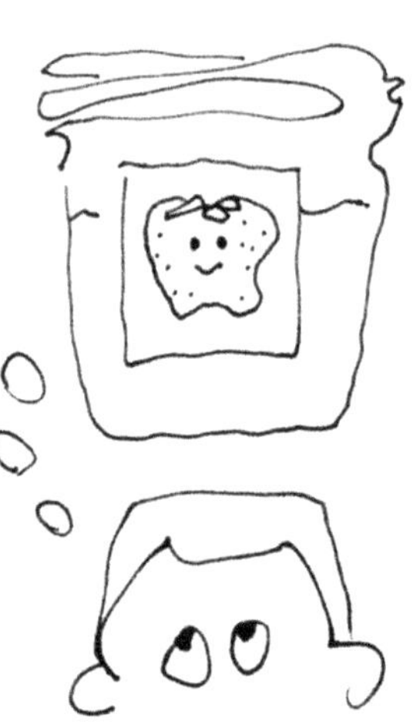

Strawberry jam
in the mind

Is plentiful
to find.

"You can almost
taste it," he said.

"Can I have some more
on my bread?"

Inside, upside,

down,

Always comes

around.

Twisting, turning

through—

From where,

it never knew.

DEF GHI...
XYZABC

A, B, C,

    through Y and Z,

All repeat

    eternally.

But if it

    never ends,

How did it, then,

    begin?

If one and one

is two,

Then what

are ones to do?

If they are still

the same,

Then why'd they

change their name?

Little candle
  burning bright—

How is it you
  reveal the night?

Extinguished now,
  I want to know,

Where is your light?
  Where did it go?

Jeeves, the philosopher,
stood by the door,

Yearning to comprehend
what it was for.

"Am I to enter it
or to come out?"

Thus he remained there,
transfixed by his doubt.

Having time can

be so hard.

Bert's fled down

the boulevard.

Madge saved some

the other day.

Where it went,

no one can say.

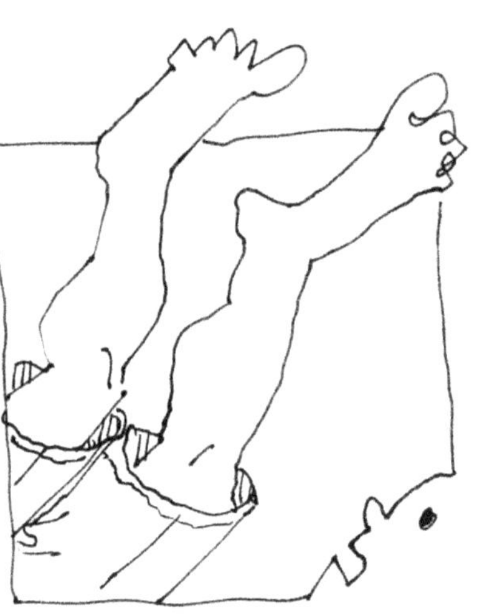

Jethro cried,

    "What shall I do?

I must have lost

    my barefoot shoe!

I took it off

    to put it on,

But that was after

    it was gone."

The farther out
    on the wheel you go,

The harder it is
    to hold on, you know.

But in the center
    there is a spot where

The wheel is still,
    it simply is there.

KO-EM 16

One is hot,

    and one is cold.

One is growing

    very old.

All together,

    they are three.

But they're not,

    it's plain to see.

Jenks called out
so clear:

"Pray, why am
I here?"

Pray said,
"Jenks, that's fair,

But—you're
over there."

Time is hanging
    on the wall.

Pacing up
    and down the hall.

Ever present,
    everywhere.

Even when I'm gone,
    it's there.

HERE LIES
? ? ? ?

After you've died,

    what is your name?

Do you believe

    it stays the same?

Your parents' choice—

    forever set?

What was your name

    before they met?

Corky and his
   sister, Bea,

Both went down
   in history.

Coming back,
   with some despair,

Said, "It's empty!
   Nothing's there."

Some folks still haven't
  conjured up why

Jenny dove in and
  swam through the sky.

Climbed up a cloud bank,
  dried in the sun.

How does one reckon
  why that was done?

Little Wilbur,

standing tall,

Saw his shadow

on the wall.

Shadow saw him

too, it seems.

Now it's even,

in his dreams.

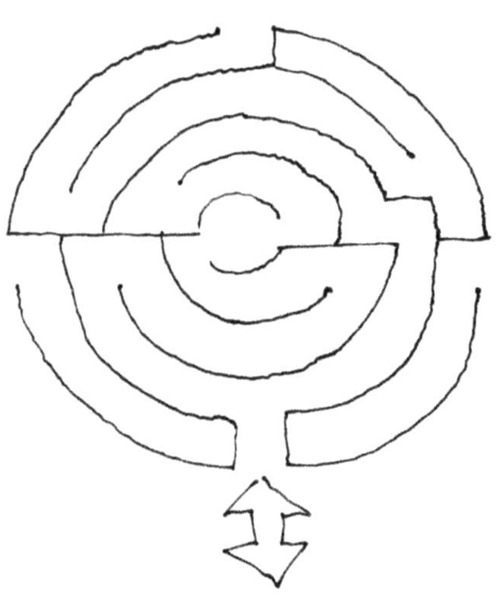

Paths are many,

    true paths are few.

What, then, is a

    seeker to do?

Finding your way home

    takes great care,

Till you see you've

    always been there.

In a world of
    give and take.

Having is the
    first mistake.

Giving seems
    the better bet—

How though,
    without causing debt?

Gibbon went
    from here to there,

Without going
    anywhere.

"Nothing's changed,"
    he said, with glee,

"No matter where
    I go, I'm me."

KO-EM 26

ROSE

A fragrant

rose

Comes

and goes.

And yet

its name

Stays

the same.

Turning in
	at night.

Turning out
	all right.

Turning round
	and round.

What is
	to be found?

The clapping hand
    stopped to rest

Thinking it had
    done its best.

"I've clapped now
    for far too long,

Silence—

    sing another song!"

The sanguine old poet
completed his verse,

And thought to himself, "Well,
it could have been worse.

There's nothing new here
that I needed to say,

So I said the old stuff,
just in a new way."

ABOUT KO-EMS

KO-EMS was written, illustrated and designed by Bodhi Bill Miller. Bill's pen name, Bodhi, pronounced *"bow-dee,"* is Sanskrit for awakening.

Bill wrote these while laid up at home for six weeks recovering from surgery. As he lay about, these couplets began streaming in, one by one, channeled from who knows where. They remain in the order they arrived—except for the preface and epilogue, which came in the middle of the process but were clearly meant to be moved to their rightful place in the queue.

After the thirtieth KO-EM arrived, the cosmic connection unplugged itself and there hasn't been one since *(with one exception: end of book)*. Honoring his intuitive process, Bill hasn't tried to concoct another one either. Otherwise, with just a few minor tweaks over the years, they are as they originally appeared.

In these distressing times, seems they might offer a whimsical smile or two for no reason.

That's the hope anyway. Enjoy!

ABOUT BODHI BILL, DMin, BCC-ret.

BILL WAS BORN artistic and imaginative, his creativity fueled by undiagnosed ADHD—which was otherwise not helpful. While art, music and writing came easy, practical life was a challenge.

Also, his affinity for Eastern spirituality didn't help much either, residing in ashrams in California and India, leading to no practical outcomes.

In midlife, Bill had a profound mystical experience at the bedside of a dying friend who was deeply distraught. Intuitively, Bill was able to gently untangle his despair. He died peacefully the next morning.

Stunned by this, Bill volunteered for hospice and discovered chaplaincy—and that, to his amazement, it was a calling. After a decade of study, he spent the next dozen years as a chaplain for the dying.

Now retired, Bill is gathering together the best of his personal musings, songs and whatnot, jotted in notebooks along the way, and offering them to whomever might find comfort, joy and meaning in them: **his legacy project.**

SONGS *of the* SPIRIT

SONGS are the bulk of my channeled creative work If you like this one, you'll probably like the rest.

Mattie Stupanek was a child prodigy poet and peace advocate. Born with a rare form of muscular dystrophy, he lived most of his life wheelchair-bound and tethered to oxygen before dying a month short of his 14th birthday.

Yet in his brief life Mattie wrote six bestselling books of poetry, and deeply touched millions—including me—sharing the uplifting power of his "Heartsongs."

Mattie's Song is my tribute to this amazing child and his vision of peace, kindness, hope and joy in a world filled with chaos, cruelty, sorrow and heartbreak.

Mattie's Song
Free YouTube link

SUBSCRIBE *to the* POST

ENJOY FREE song videos as they are completed, individual KO-EM videos, stories, spiritual musings and announcements on new books and CDs.

As much as possible, I offer a free digital version of everything I produce—although tangible also has its place. I do need a little income to keep the operation going.

The Post is published every Saturday afternoon *(hence the name)* and is intended to offer a small spark of inspiration in these dark, dystopian times.

Subscribe

BodhiBill.com

BONUS KO-EM

Showed up, unannounced,
while I was producing this book.

My Grandpa died
    in grammer school.

T'was just a lad,
    it seemed so cruel.

He's with me now,
    so I don't mourn.

Because of him,
    I was not born.

miller & muse

STORIES and SONGS for the SPIRITUALLY CURIOUS

Follow Bodhi Bill

BodhiBill.com